LA MISIÓN DE DARTH MAUL

ACE LANDERS ILUSTRADO POR DAVID WHITE

...GO, THE LEGO LOGO, THE BRICK AND KNOB
...FIGURATIONS AND THE MINIFIGURE ARE
...DEMARKS OF THE LEGO GROUP. © 2015 THE
...GO GROUP.
...& TM 2015 LUCASFILM LTD.

...NSLATION COPYRIGHT © 2015 BY SCHOLASTIC INC.

...RIGHTS RESERVED. PUBLISHED BY SCHOLASTIC
..., PUBLISHERS SINCE 1920. SCHOLASTIC, SCHOLASTIC
...ESPAÑOL, AND ASSOCIATED LOGOS ARE TRADEMARKS
.../OR REGISTERED TRADEMARKS OF SCHOLASTIC INC.

THE PUBLISHER DOES NOT HAVE ANY CONTROL
OVER AND DOES NOT ASSUME ANY RESPONSIBILITY
FOR AUTHOR OR THIRD-PARTY WEBSITES OR THEIR
CONTENT.

NO PART OF THIS PUBLICATION MAY BE REPRODUCED,
STORED IN A RETRIEVAL SYSTEM, OR TRANSMITTED
IN ANY FORM OR BY ANY MEANS, ELECTRONIC,
MECHANICAL, PHOTOCOPYING, RECORDING, OR
OTHERWISE, WITHOUT WRITTEN PERMISSION OF THE
PUBLISHER. FOR INFORMATION REGARDING PERMISSION,
WRITE TO SCHOLASTIC INC. ATTENTION: PERMISSIONS
DEPARTMENT, 557 BROADWAY, NEW YORK, NY 10012.

THIS BOOK IS A WORK OF FICTION. NAMES,
CHARACTERS, PLACES, AND INCIDENTS ARE EITHER
THE PRODUCT OF THE AUTHOR'S IMAGINATION OR ARE
USED FICTITIOUSLY, AND ANY RESEMBLANCE TO ACTUAL
PERSONS, LIVING OR DEAD, BUSINESS ESTABLISHMENTS,
EVENTS, OR LOCALES IS ENTIRELY COINCIDENTAL.

ISBN 978-0-545-85178-7

10 9 8 7 6 5 4 3   15 16 17 18 19/0

PRINTED IN THE U.S.A.   40
FIRST SCHOLASTIC SPANISH PRINTING, SEPTEMBER 2015

SCHOLASTIC INC.

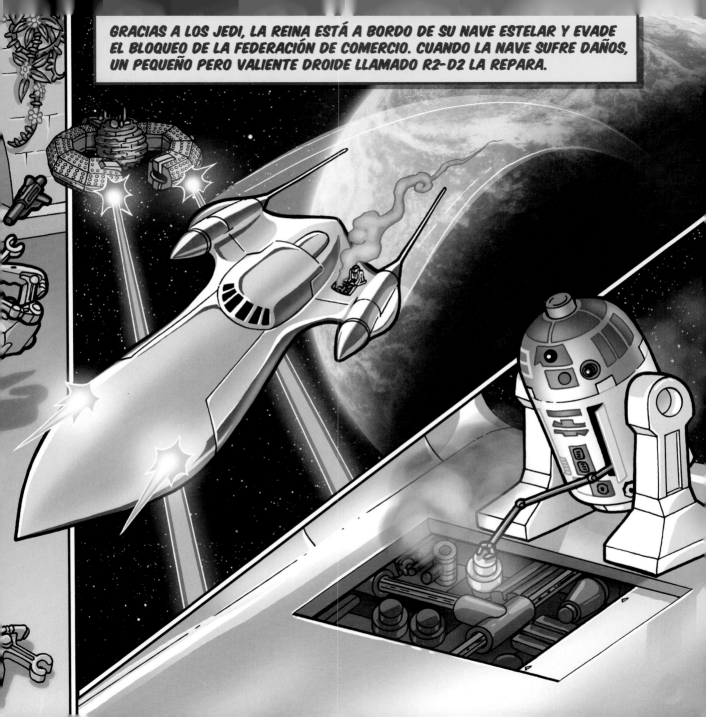

GRACIAS A LOS JEDI, LA REINA ESTÁ A BORDO DE SU NAVE ESTELAR Y EVADE EL BLOQUEO DE LA FEDERACIÓN DE COMERCIO. CUANDO LA NAVE SUFRE DAÑOS, UN PEQUEÑO PERO VALIENTE DROIDE LLAMADO R2-D2 LA REPARA.

EL DUELO ES A TODA VELOCIDAD.

DARTH MAUL Y QUI-GON SE BATEN, SE ESQUIVAN Y SE ATACAN EL UNO AL OTRO.
EL RUIDO QUE HACEN LOS SABLES DE LUZ AL CHOCAR CORTA EL AIRE DEL DESIERTO.

LA REINA VUELA DE REGRESO A NABOO PARA ENFRENTAR AL EJÉRCITO DE LA FEDERACIÓN DE COMERCIO, PERO DARTH MAUL ESTÁ A LA ESPERA DE LOS CABALLEROS JEDI.

QUI-GON Y OBI-WAN ATACAN A DARTH MAUL. MAUL PELEA DANDO SALTOS Y VOLTERETAS Y LOGRA GOLPEAR A OBI-WAN Y TUMBARLO. LUEGO METE A QUI-GON EN UN CLÓSET PARA PODER PELEAR UNO A UNO CON OBI-WAN.

CERRAR

POR FIN LOS HÉROES PUEDEN CELEBRAR.

E Lan Spanish
Landers, Ace.
La misiÃ³n de Darth Maul